Hubble

A BOOK OF WITCHES & WIZARDS

Bubble

BY JOHN PATIENCE

DERRYDALE BOOKS
New York

The Witch Next Door

Amy's father had been given a new job in a new town and the family had just moved house. It was all rather frightening for Amy. She had left all her old friends behind and the children who were playing in the street didn't seem to want to know her. She went out and stood at the garden gate, watching them and hoping that they would invite her over to play, but they didn't. One of them even began to make faces at her and call her names. When she went down to the shop for her mother, two big boys jumped out at her from an alleyway, making her drop the shopping. Then they chased her all the way home.

Amy's mother did her best to make her feel better, but that night Amy lay in bed wishing she was back in her old house surrounded by her old friends. Then something happened to make her forget her troubles. She heard a funny sort of noise outside her window. Tiptoeing across her room, she peeped out through the curtains and saw the strangest thing. The woman who lived next door was flying around the sky on her vacuum cleaner! The first time she had seen that woman Amy had guessed that there was something funny about her – she had spiky red hair, wore weird make-up and peculiar clothes. "Of course," whispered Amy, "she's a witch!"

The next morning at breakfast Amy told her mother and father about the witch next door, but they just laughed and told her not to be so silly. "There's no such thing as witches," said her mother. "Look, there's a letter for the lady next door. The postman delivered it to our house by mistake. Take it round for me, there's a good girl.' Well, Amy was not too happy about that, but she did as she was told. She took the letter, which was addressed to Mrs. Moon, and knocked on her door. The loud music which had been playing in the house was turned off and, through the coloured glass in the front door, Amy could see the witch coming down the hallway. Then the door opened. "Hello. You're the little girl next door, aren't you?" said the witch. "Is that letter for me? That postman! He's a real daydreamer. Come in – we'll get to know each other." Amy was completely tongue-tied, but she followed the witch into the house. And a very funny house it was, too, with all sorts of strange posters and paintings on the walls, and all kinds of junk lying around everywhere. "Don't mind the mess," said the witch cheerily. "I'll get around to tidying it up some day." And she led Amy into the kitchen and there was the witch's black cat, curled up on a chair. But the room was warm and friendly, and Amy's fears began to melt away. Maybe Mrs. Moon was a good witch, a white witch. There was a wonderful smell in the kitchen of newly baked bread. Mrs. Moon cut a big slice off the loaf, spread lots of butter and jam on it and gave it to Amy. "Try that," she said. "I think it's the best I've ever baked." Amy took a bite and at that moment, as if by magic, she and the witch became the best of friends and Amy was telling Mrs. Moon all kinds of things about where she came from and how she couldn't make friends with the other children in the street.

"Don't worry," said Mrs. Moon. "You'll have no more trouble. I've got something special for you. Here it is. It's a magic woolly hat – I knitted it myself. When you put this hat on your head you will turn into a little monster and you'll never be afraid of anyone again. After all, no-one chases monsters, do they? But be a good monster – don't go round frightening everybody, will you?" "No, I wouldn't do that," promised Amy. Then she put on the woolly hat, turned into a monster and went home.

"Hello, Mum. I'm a monster," said Amy. "So you are,"

said Amy's mother. "Would you go down to the shop for some washing powder dear?" "Sure," said Amy. She knew that no-one would chase her now, so she was feeling pleased with herself and full of confidence. In the street she smiled a great big monster smile and the other children smiled back at her. "Hi!" they said. "Do you want to play with us?" "Later," said Amy. "I'm a monster and I'm going down to the shop for my Mum." Being a monster was really great – the best thing ever! Amy leapt up into the air, swung around a road sign and ran off down the pavement.

As Amy was on her way back from the shop, the two big boys tried to scare her again, but she gave a terrible, fierce monster roar and they both ran away. After that she went to play with the other children. They thought that they would like to be monsters too, so they all pretended. Then there were lots of little monsters leaping around all over the place though, of course, Amy was the best because she was wearing her magic monster hat.

Now Amy was happy. She had made lots of new friends, but her very best friend of all was Mrs. Moon. That night she saw her whizzing around the sky on her vacuum cleaner again, sucking up the stars as if they were crumbs on the carpet. She tapped on the window and waved and Mrs. Moon waved back. Then Amy put on her monster hat, curled up in bed and fell asleep.

Esmeralda

smeralda was a witch's cat,
But found it none too easy.
Looping loops and swooping swoops –
It made her feel quite queasy.
And one wild night, by pale moonlight,
Green with travel sickness,
She lost her grip, began to slip
And found herself broomstickless.
Where she fell it's strange to tell.
It's weird to be relating.
Down my chimney pot the feline shot,
Her speed accelerating.
Now, it's no joke to be awoke
By wild things from the chimney.
My heart went BUMP, it made me jump,
It made me shout, "By Jimmeny!"
But you'd never guess her origins
From looking at her now.
She's just like any other cat,
The same purr and meow.
There's just that look she gives you,
The one that makes you quiver,
Shudder, shake, turn cold and quake,
Tremble, squirm and shiver!

Good Neighbours

t the end of Badger Lane there stood two adjoining cottages. A witch lived in one of them and her next-door-neighbour was a wizard. They had never been on good terms, in fact, to be quite blunt, they hated each other. The witch was forever brewing up really foul-smelling potions and those smells always found their way into the wizard's house.

One morning, when there was a very bad smell in the air, the wizard noticed that the witch was out in her garden, presumably collecting some more rubbish to add to her concoction. Stalking out into his own garden, the wizard leaned across the fence and said, "Oh, look! There's a lovely slimy snail, and there's a nice juicy worm, and goodness me, don't miss that fat little frog!" "Keep your remarks to yourself, you old fool," sneered the witch. "Keep your smells to yourself, then," shouted the wizard. "You horrible old bat!" "Old bat, am I? At least I don't keep people awake all night, chanting stupid spells and dancing around like a demented donkey. You're a useless wizard, anyway. You couldn't cast a proper spell to save your life!" This was too much for the wizard. "We'll see about that," he muttered darkly. "We'll see about that."

The wizard pored over his spell books all night long. It was ages since he had worked any really powerful magic.

Mostly, he earned his living by vanishing warts from the end of people's noses and that sort of thing. But now he was looking for something special, something extremely impressive and eventually he found it.

The next morning he confronted the witch over the garden fence again. "Couldn't cast a spell to save my life, eh?" he said. "Watch this, then." And he began to chant something like this:

> "Elgnuj, elgnuj, round about
> Mumbo jumbo, inside out,
> Tac to oppih, oppih pot,
> Turn around and watchagot?"

Then, in an instant, it happened. The witch's garden was transformed into a tropical jungle and her cat, which had been toying with a mouse, was changed into (of all things) a hippopotamus! The witch was beside herself with rage.

She waved her wand in the air and shrieked out some bizarre magic spell of her own. The wizard's beard turned green, his ears grew long and furry like a donkey's. Then he blew up like a balloon and floated up into the air.

Well, that was the beginning of the magic war. Soon the witch and the wizard were casting all kinds of spells on each other. First, the witch's broomstick caught fire.

The wizard's chair jumped up and ran away with him. Then a plague of nasty little nameless creatures came down the chimney, chased the witch all around her house and pinched her black and blue.

This sort of nonsense couldn't go on for ever, of course, and it happened that they both decided at the very same time to put an end to it with the very best spell they could conjure up. "I'll show the old crone," thought the wizard. "I'll teach the silly old fool," muttered the witch. And while the wizard scoured his magic books for a spell to end all spells, the witch threw everything she could find into her bubbling cauldron.

The wizard looked pale-faced and grim as he stood in his garden the following morning. He stretched out his arms towards the witch and began to chant the terrible spell he had learned:

"All things black and horrible,
Mischief from the night,
Slimy things, and grimy things
And rhymes that aren't quite right,
Toothache and the collywobbles,
Mumps and the chickenpox,
Boils and warts and thingummybobs
And nasty-smelling socks."

As he spoke, coloured smoke started to pour out from his fingertips, and the witch realised that she had better hurry up and work her own magic. She took a bottle filled with her magic potion from under her cape and, taking off the stopper, threw it at the wizard. "Magic, do your stuff!" she cried. And if a drop of the potion had touched the wizard it might well have turned him into a toad, but it didn't. The witch's and the wizard's magic met and mixed in mid air and something remarkable happened. There was a smash, a crash, a splash and a flash and a terrible monster appeared. It had four great bulging eyes, terrible claws and a mouth full of horrible, yellow teeth. And it roared like a lion. It smashed down the fence and chased the terrified witch and wizard all around their gardens. Around and around they ran with the dreadful monster rushing after them, until, at last, completely exhausted and imagining that at any minute they would both be gobbled up, they fell down on their knees. "I'm sorry," panted the witch. "It's all my fault." "No, no. It's my fault," puffed the wizard. "I'm sorry."

"Sorry, sorry, sorry. Did you say sorry?" bellowed the monster, turning horribly pale. "Yes, that's right, sorry," cried the wizard, realising that he had discovered the magic word. "Sorry, sorry, sorry!" shouted the witch and the wizard together, dancing around and hugging each other. Then the monster began to shake and tremble quite uncontrollably. He shook so violently that he shook himself to pieces and crumbled into a pile of dust.

From that day on, the witch and the wizard became the very best of friends and often popped into each other's houses for a cup of tea and to exchange spells.

The Frog Prince

Oh, a happy little frog, was I,
Sitting in my ditch,
Croaking at the clear blue sky,
When along came a wicked witch.
She cast an evil spell on me,
To think of it makes me wince,
She turned me in an instant
Into a handsome prince.
Now I must leave my froggy friends
It's time to go, I guess.
I must bid farewell to contentment,
And marry some silly princess!

Simple Jack and the Wizard

There was once a poor boy named Jack who earned his living as a street musician. He wore tattered, ragged clothes, but a happy smile. The rich people of the town laughed at Jack. They jeered at him from their coaches as they rode by. They called him "simple." But Jack didn't mind. He made enough money to buy himself food and drink and keep a roof over his head.

One day a wizard came to the town where Jack lived and, standing in the square, he threw his arms into the air and brought down a tremendous bolt of lightning. "I am your ruler," he shouted. "From this moment you are all my slaves. You will work for me. I will see that you have all the food you need and I will give you clothes to wear, but if you do not obey me, I will kill you all!"

It seemed that there was very little choice. The wizard must be obeyed. He commanded the townsfolk to build him a great tower of glittering gold in the square and kept them working at it day and night. Then, when it was completed, he took up residence and from its high balcony he was able to keep watch on the entire town to see that no-one disobeyed his laws. These were some of the laws:

There will be no smiling or laughing.

Children will not play games in the streets, and

There will be absolutely NO music.

Well, the people obeyed all these terrible laws and the wizard gave them food to eat and clothes to wear, but the food which he conjured out of thin air tasted of nothing at

all and did not satisfy anyone's hunger, and the clothes he gave them were drab grey and didn't keep out the cold.

At last the townsfolk couldn't stand it any longer. They gathered at the golden tower to confront the wizard. "We are unhappy," they moaned. "Your laws are stupid and pointless." This made the wizard extremely angry and, with a sweep of his arm, he magically summoned up three great trolls, who threatened everyone, and patrolled the town to make sure that no-one else got any silly ideas about being happy.

But what had become of Simple Jack? Well now, I doubt if there was anyone in that whole, unhappy town more unhappy than poor Jack. Now that he was no longer allowed to play his pipe in the streets, his cheerful smile had disappeared like the sun behind a big, grey cloud. But Jack had courage and he decided that he must go to see the

wizard. "After all," thought Jack, "I have nothing to lose. The wizard has made life so miserable that it is hardly worth living."

Jack knocked loudly on the door of the golden tower and soon the wizard appeared. "What do you want?" he growled. "Why aren't you working with the other townsfolk?" The wizard had commanded that everyone should begin working at a great carving of himself which was to be hewn out of the side of a mountain which overlooked the town. They had been slaving away at it for months, watched over by the three trolls. "I'm not interested in carving statues. I want to play my pipe in the streets the way I used to," replied Jack bravely. At this, the wizard roared with anger and, chanting a spell, magicked into being, a terrifying, fire-breathing thingummybob. Anyone else would have turned and run, but Jack stood his ground. He had begun to realise something about the wizard. His magic was all illusion, it had no substance. The food he gave did not fill the people's stomachs or satisfy their hunger. The clothes did not keep them warm. And, come to think of it, that bolt of lightning he had brought down had hit a dog and it hadn't even scratched it.

Jack decided to put his idea to the test. Putting his pipe to his lips, he began to play and as the forbidden music filled the air, the monster began to shrink smaller and smaller and smaller until eventually it was no bigger than a mouse, at which point it took fright and ran away. (If anyone is interested, I think it was caught and eaten by a cat.) "Go away or I'll, I'll, I'll … I don't know what I'll do!" screamed the wizard. "You're just a fraud," said Jack and he started to laugh. The wizard was mortified, no-one had ever dared to laugh at him before. The sound stabbed him like a knife. He let out a horrible scream and, beginning at his toes and working upwards, he began to fade away, until … at last only his head remained, floating in the air. And then that, too, turned into a mist and was blown away. And the wizard was never seen or heard of again.

The trolls disappeared along with the wizard and everyone was free again. The children played games in the streets. People laughed and joked and – best of all as far as he was concerned – Jack was able to go back to playing his pipe. Actually, the townsfolk wanted to make him Lord Mayor and dress him up in fine clothes, but he refused. You might think that was stupid of him, but he was happy just the way he was. And as a matter of fact, people stopped calling him Simple Jack after that and named him Happy Jack instead.